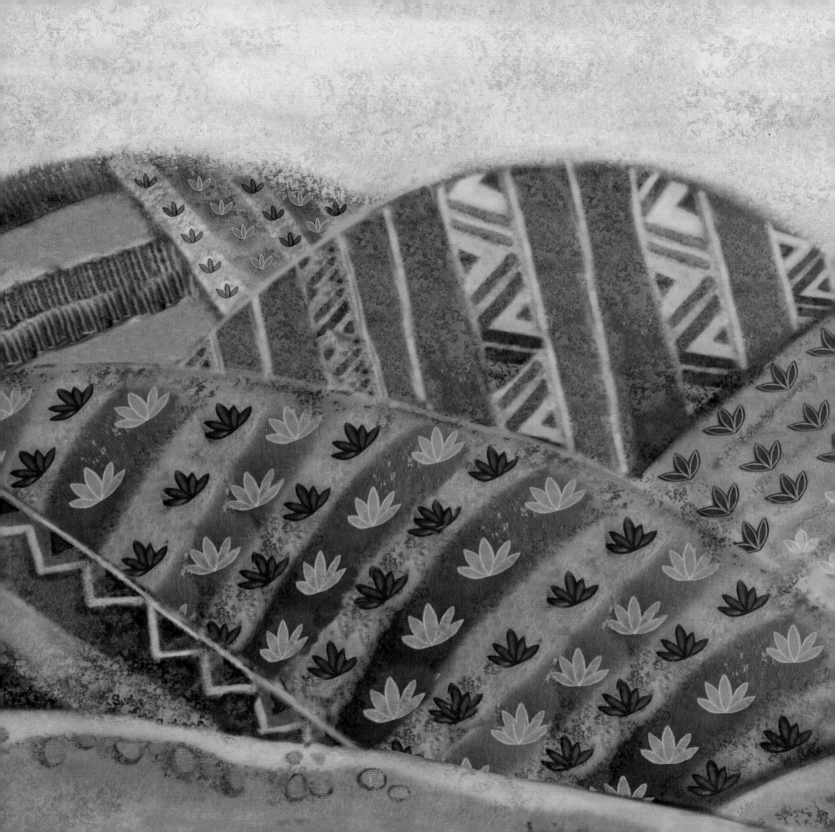

A gift to

_____

From

_____

With joy on this date

_____

DEDICATION

For Jesus, the Giver of Life
"In your presence there is fullness of joy."—Psalm 16:11

For the Kenyan mamas, who freely give of themselves every day:
Agnes, Sally, Ednah, and Vanessa.

For Tom, Anna, Abigail, Micah, Ezra, and Caleb,
a few of God's greatest gifts to me.

Copyright © 2017 by April Graney
Published by B&H Publishing Group, Nashville, Tennessee
ISBN: 978-1-4627-4099-4

Dewey Decimal Classification: C967.62
Subject Heading: KENYA \ HAPPINESS \ CHRISTIAN LIFE

All rights reserved. Printed in Shenzhen, Guangdong, China, in July 2018.
2 3 4 5 6 7 8   22 21 20 19 18

THE MARVELOUS MUD HOUSE

APRIL GRANEY

illustrations by Alida Massari

On the edge of a lush mountain in Kenya sat a marvelous mud house where George and his mother lived. What made this mud house marvelous was the marvelous thing that happened there.

Each morning, as the sun flooded the Great Rift Valley below, George searched the terraced garden for corn, mangoes, and potatoes while Mama George milked the goat. Then they loaded their baskets on their backs and began their long walk to the village.

Down, down, down one side of their mountain and up, up, up the side of the next mountain they walked. And every day, Mama George sang,

"We're rich, my son, rich in love, strength, and life!
The Giver of these hears every cry!
Let's lift up our hands to the God who provides."

One morning, George could hear the children singing from the schoolhouse.

"Mama," he said with a sigh, "all my friends are in school. I want to go too, but how will we pay the fees?"

Mama George raised her eyes and replied, "Let's keep working, George. God will provide."

Far away on the edge of the Oklahoma woods sat a hungry ranch house where the Smith family lived. What made this house hungry was the feeling of always wanting more.

The five Smith children—Olivia, Ruth, Thomas, Tucker, and Ben—had toy trucks and trains, footballs and board games, pretty dolls and stuffed bears, one brown-and-white beagle, and one whopping big car.

But clean-up time brought weeping and whines. And with closets overflowing with toys, they still begged their parents, "Oh, please, buy us a little bit more!"

Then one day, an adventure began. The Smith family hopped on a plane and flew up in the sky, over the land, and across the ocean. . . .

. . . to Kenya!

10

There they saw a new world full of yawning rhinos, graceful
giraffes, playful monkeys, and mischievous baboons. They saw
boys selling bananas and girls carrying water on their heads.

And there, in a village market, the Smith family met George
and his mother.

Every day, the Smiths stopped to buy corn and chat with George and Mama George. The youngest Smith, Ben, gathered the courage to ask, "Where do you live? Is it very far?"

Mama George leaned over with a smile. "We can show you! Please come to our house for dinner."

So down, down, down one side of the mountain and up, up, up the side of the next mountain went the two families.

As they passed the schoolhouse, Ben asked, "Is that your school, George?"

His new friend shrugged. "I hope to go there someday, if we get the school fees."

"God will provide," Mama George reminded. As they walked, she taught the Smith family her song,

"We're rich, my friends, rich in love, strength, and life!
The Giver of these hears every cry!
Let's lift up our hands to the God who provides."

Soon they reached the marvelous mud house. Ben was surprised. "But, George, where's your house?" he asked.

"Right here!" George replied. "Mama George and I built it ourselves!"

"But, George, where's your car?"

"We use our feet!" said George.

"But, George, where are your games?"

George said, "I'll show you!" He quickly began showing how much fun it was to play hide-and-seek among the corn and mango trees and make up games with pebbles and banana leaves.

When it was time for dinner, both families gathered inside the marvelous mud house. There they sat, knees touching as they savored plantain stew, ugali, and chapatis. George passed around sweet, fried mandazis.

A lantern flickered on nine smiling faces, and the walls rang with laughter. With full bellies, the Smith children looked 'round in wonder. In the mud house, to be surrounded by joy and love was enough, much more than the accumulation of stuff.

That night, Ben's eyes watered
as he hugged Mama George goodbye.
"Asante,"

he said in his best Swahili accent.
"Thank you."

The next day, as the Smiths flew back across the ocean, Ben thought about the marvelous mud house and how full it seemed—full of fun and laughter and friendship. Full of Mama George's faith and her joyful songs. And suddenly he remembered what it felt like to be full too.

Back at home, something seemed different at the hungry ranch house. The children rarely asked for more things at the store. And they all hugged each other a little bit more.

"We don't need so much stuff," they said. "A little is enough. Let's help George go to school instead!"

Olivia said, "I can babysit."

Ruth said, "I can have a bake sale."

Thomas said, "I can rake leaves."

Mom and Dad said, "We can get a smaller car."

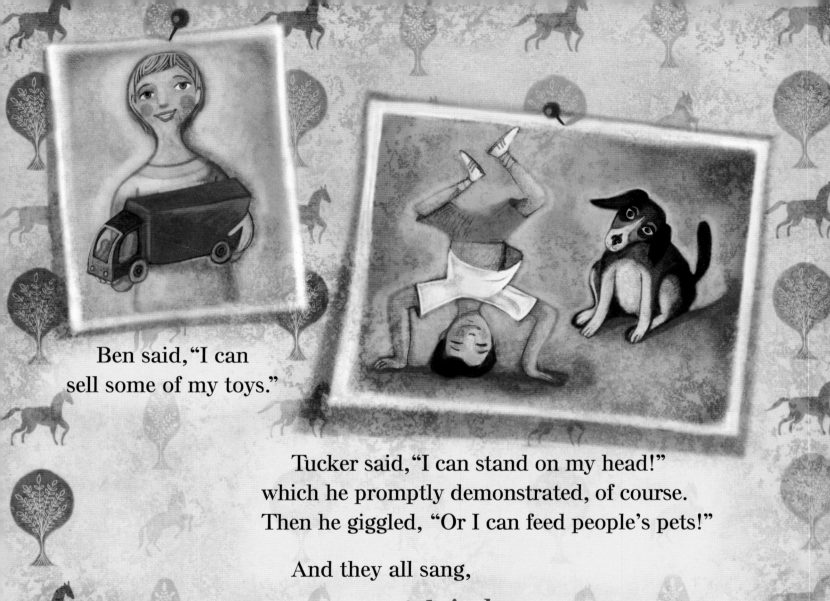

Ben said, "I can sell some of my toys."

Tucker said, "I can stand on my head!"
which he promptly demonstrated, of course.
Then he giggled, "Or I can feed people's pets!"

And they all sang,

"We're rich in Christ, rich in love, strength, and life!
The Giver of these hears every cry!
Let's lift up our hands to the God who provides."

Back in Kenya, George still thought about going to school. He planted more and more corn, but he and Mama George still did not have the money to pay school fees. He wondered if Mama was right to trust God to help.

But Mama George continued to pray. "Lord, will You help us?"

Then one day, Mama George received
a letter from far away. She carefully
opened it and read, "You taught us so
much, and we want to bless you. Please
use this money to send George to school.
Your friends, the Smiths."

Mama George began to cry—not tears of sadness, but of joy. She skipped down, down, down the side of the mountain and leapt up, up, up the side of the next mountain, hurrying to find George.

"Mama, what's wrong? Why do you run so fast?" George asked.

Mama George read the letter aloud. "George, God has provided for us!" she cried.

"I'm going to school!" George squealed. He wrapped his arms tight 'round his mother and let out a great big whoop and a holler!

Two houses that night rang with laughter and dance, one marvelous mud house on a mountain, and one happy house on a ranch!

REMEMBER:

But godliness with contentment is great gain. — 1 Timothy 6:6

READ:

Read Psalm 90:14. This verse asks God to fill us up with His love so we can sing for joy! He has given us life in Him, but sometimes we forget and instead search for happiness in the things we own or accomplish, none of which make us truly happy. God wants to satisfy us with His love instead! He loves us so much that He sent His Son, Jesus, to die for us. Jesus said, "I have come that they may have life, and have it to the full!" (John 10:10 NIV). He wants to save us from our sins and give us a full life in Him. When we find our contentment and joy in Jesus, we can then love and care for others who are in need.

THINK:

1. Tell about a time when someone helped you. How did that make you feel? Was that person showing love, like Jesus?
2. In the story, how did Mama George and George help the Smith family? How did the Smiths then help George and Mama George?
3. The Smiths learned that joy and faith were true riches and that they did not need to own so much stuff to be happy. Would you rather have a life full of stuff or a life full of joy and faith? Why?
4. What can you share with others? How can you help earn money to give to others in need, as Ben and his family did? How can you share joy and faith as Mama George did?
5. Mama George had great faith that God could hear her and could answer her prayers. Do you know that God also hears you when you pray to Him? What needs can you share with Him?

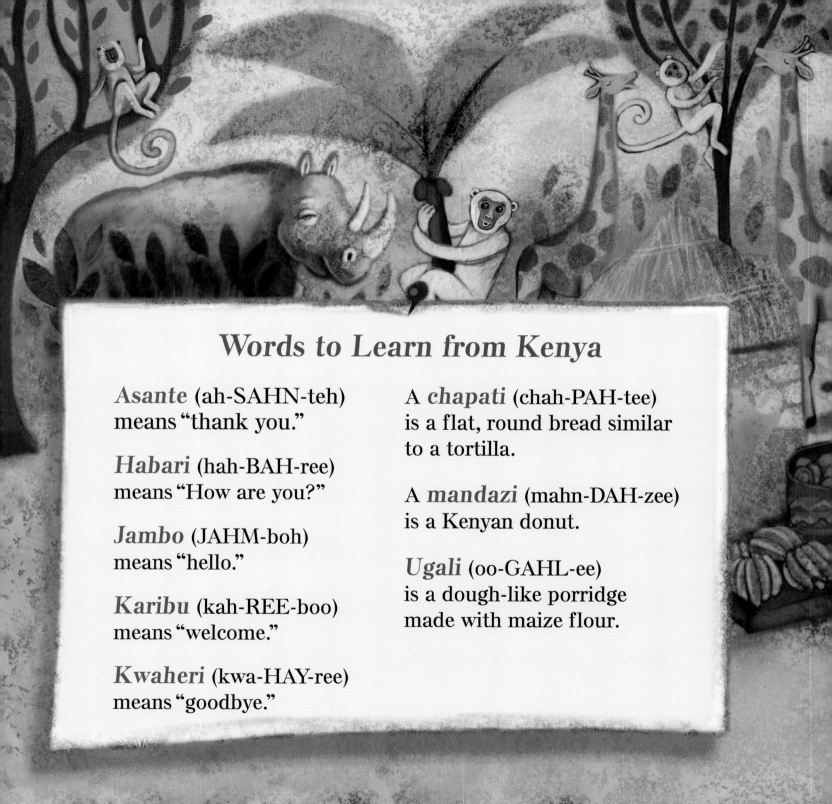

Words to Learn from Kenya

Asante (ah-SAHN-teh) means "thank you."

Habari (hah-BAH-ree) means "How are you?"

Jambo (JAHM-boh) means "hello."

Karibu (kah-REE-boo) means "welcome."

Kwaheri (kwa-HAY-ree) means "goodbye."

A **chapati** (chah-PAH-tee) is a flat, round bread similar to a tortilla.

A **mandazi** (mahn-DAH-zee) is a Kenyan donut.

Ugali (oo-GAHL-ee) is a dough-like porridge made with maize flour.

artwork of George's village
by Abigail Cheboi, age 12, Kenya